Stealing Haven

A Jamie Richmond Mystery

Mark Love

Stealing Haven
A Jamie Richmond Novella

ISBN: (ebook) 978-1-953335-69-2
(print) 978-1-953335-70-8

Inkspell Publishing
207 Moonglow Circle #101
Murrells Inlet, SC 29576

Cover art by: Fantasia Frog Designs

OTHER BOOKS BY MARK LOVE

THE JAMIE RICHMOND SERIES

"DEVIOUS"

"VANISHING ACT"

"FLEEING BEAUTY"

THE JEFFERSON CHENE SERIES

"WHY 319?"

"YOUR TURN TO DIE"

*****COMING SOON*****

THE WAYWARD PATH

DEDICATION

For Kim,
Let's take a little stroll along the beach

CHAPTER ONE

I didn't want to move.

Moving would convince me I wasn't asleep. The cool breeze caressing my bare skin was not the touch of some mysterious lover who appeared when the lights went out. He treated me like a princess, understanding how the slight nuzzle behind my knee had a very unladylike effect on me, how with just tiny encouragement, the little bits I wore would disappear in a heartbeat. How…

"Jamie! We have to get moving," a sultry voice said. "You're going to sleep away the day. We could have stayed home and done that."

I waved a hand to push her away. Maybe the guy who'd been caressing my knee was still there. *He was.* I could tell by the wet tongue stroking my leg. I jerked awake and rolled over. Instantly, I was greeted by a mass of fur and several sloppy kisses. Satisfied, the dog moved away in pursuit of someone else to bother and I threw my arm up over my face.

"Linda, can't you control Logan?" My voice came out muffled.

She flopped down beside me and tugged my arm down. "Of course, I can. He was simply following orders. We have miles of soft sandy beach out there, just waiting for us. Blue skies and enough wind to fill a sail. And who knows how many handsome men may be pining for us at this very moment?"

I pried open both eyes to see if she was serious. She was. Then I took a good look at her. Part of me wanted to smack her, just because. She'd gotten the same four hours of sleep I had, yet, Linda could have stepped out of the pages of a fashion magazine. Her luxurious dark curly hair was pulled back with a headband. The waves swept across her shoulders like gentle wings. Two weeks into June and she sported a bronzed tan I could never achieve. Her curvaceous body and shapely legs could make a gay man stand up and take notice. But it was her angelic face that always closed the deal. She rarely wore makeup. She didn't need it.

Giving my head a shake to chase away the remnants of my dream, I realized she was already dressed for the beach in a modest red bikini with a white lacy blouse as a cover-up. Like that'd reduce the attention she'd draw.

"Come on. We're wasting sunshine."

"How long have you been awake?" I mumbled.

"Fifteen minutes. The coffee should be ready." There was no disguising the enthusiasm in her voice. "Get ready, or I'm tempted to leave you behind."

"I need more than coffee."

"There's an adorable little bakery between here and the beach. I'll buy you a muffin."

"What the hell." I slid off the bed and trudged to the bathroom.

God, she's so annoying, at times. As gorgeous as a Hollywood icon and able to bounce out of bed ready to face the world with minimal effort, some days, I hated her. She gave the dog his daily praise, as I splashed cold water on my face and raked a comb through my red locks. In the background, I heard the screen door slam as the dog slipped outside. Shedding the camisole and panties I'd worn to bed, I stepped into a bright green bikini. From my bag in the room, I dug out a threadbare man's dress shirt and slipped it on as a cover. Exiting the bedroom, Linda handed me a cardboard cup of coffee. Over one shoulder was a large straw bag filled with a beach towel, sunscreen, an extra pair of shorts, a floppy hat and a book. I had one just like it sitting beside the door. I grabbed mine as we walked outside.

Logan sprawled in the shade. Sitting on a campstool was a short, stocky man with a weathered face. Thin wisps of grey hair danced in the breeze off the lake. In front of him was an easel with a tattered canvas. He turned slightly as we approached.

"Do you mind watching the dog while we're at the beach, Uncle Jake?" Linda asked.

He pointed the end of the paintbrush at her. "Nah, the dog's better company than you two. I've trained him to fetch me a beer."

"You can't be serious," I said.

Jake winked a pale-brown eye at me. "About which part?"

"The beer. You love our company."

"Shows what you know." He twisted toward Logan and made a clicking noise with his false teeth. The dog jumped up and trotted to the corner of the house. He stuck his nose into an old galvanized tub then pulled back with a can of beer clutched in his mouth. Logan returned and stood beside Jake. Chuckling with delight, Jake eased it from the dog's mouth. From a pocket of his paint-splattered shirt, he withdrew a dog biscuit. Logan took the treat and returned to his spot beneath the tree. With a grin, Jake opened the beer and took a healthy slug.

"It's eight-thirty in the morning and you're drinking beer. You're corrupting my baby," Linda said. She struggled to keep her tone serious.

"The dog's a Golden Retriever. It's in his blood to fetch."

"Don't give him any beer," Linda admonished.

Jake fluttered a hand at her. "Go on. Have fun. And don't be bringing any lecherous boys back here with you. Dinner's at six."

Linda winked at me. She leaned in on Jake's right side. I leaned in on the left. Simultaneously we kissed him on the respective cheek. I noticed the sparkle in his eye as we headed out.

"Is he really your uncle?"

"No. Jake's more like an old family friend. He and his wife were very close with my parents. We visited them every summer but it's been years since I've been back. He retired about the same time my dad did. Within a year, his wife passed away. Jake grumbles once in a while about moving south, but I doubt it will ever happen. He loves the lake."

By the time we found the bakery, my coffee was gone. After devouring a cranberry orange muffin, I felt a little more human. South Haven is a popular vacation spot with people from Chicago as well as the Detroit area. We wandered through the town and strolled down the long path, following the channel that led from the marina. Boats of all different shapes, sizes and colors dotted the docks. Many of them were buttoned up. The owners were probably counting the hours until they could return during the evening or on the weekend. As we neared the end of the channel, Linda veered off to the left and the great expanse of sandy beach. I stopped in my tracks as though hypnotized.

"What's wrong?"

As far as my eyes could see, Lake Michigan sprawled before us. I'd been here a few times before, but the majesty of the Great Lake never failed to overwhelm me. It seemed like it should be a whole lot farther than a four-hour drive from my home near Motown. The green flags gently rippled from the pier and caught my attention, indicating it was safe to go into the water without fear of a rip current carrying you away.

"C'mon, let's go find a cozy spot on the beach. I want to dip my toes in the water."

I gave myself a shake and followed her. "What's the matter, afraid your bikini will melt if you get it wet?"

She waved her fingers over her shoulder. Linda continued walking farther away from the pier which jutted out alongside the marina's canal. From where I stood, I saw a steady flow of tourists trudging out to take pictures in front of the lighthouse. Fortunately, the beach wasn't as jammed as it'd be on a weekend. Linda paused long enough to kick off her sandals, scoop them up with one hand and wiggle her toes in the sand. She did it gracefully. When I tried to mimic her moves, I nearly fell on my ass. Hopping on one foot, I managed to pull off my footwear. As I jammed them into my bag, I watched her move along. Even trudging through the shifting sands, her hips swayed as if she were dancing. I wondered if there was anything she did where she looked clumsy.

Linda found the perfect spot at least twenty feet away from anyone else. Kneeling on the sand, she spread out her towel and anchored it down at the corners with her sandals and her straw bag. Shedding the cover up, she rubbed sunscreen along her shoulders, arms and legs.

"I thought you were going to swim."

"It's the waterproof kind. Better safe than sunburnt. Lord knows, your skin will burn." She tossed the bottle toward me. Quickly, I applied it.

With our spot secured and sunscreen on, we didn't wait a moment longer. The sun beat down on us with nary a cloud in sight. My toes hit the water and a chill raced through me.

"It's ice water!"

"It's Lake Michigan, Jamie." Smart ass. I knew exactly where we were.

"Feels more like Lake Superior." The northernmost lake rarely warmed above freezing.

Linda gave me a disgusted look and stepped further into the water. Together we walked out until it was waist deep. In the distance, a number of people rushed across the water on kiteboards, letting the wind fill their odd shaped sails. I watched one execute several flips and turns, expertly working the breeze. Linda scraped a fingernail on my shoulder.

"Race you to that buoy."

"What boy?" I smiled.

She pushed me. As I fell, I saw her dive and swim toward a marker that bobbed about thirty feet ahead. Laughing, I took off after her. There was a gradual drop off from the beach so I could have waded out to it, but it was more fun to swim. She stood there, hands on her hips like Wonder Woman.

"I've been waiting."

"For me?"

She shook her head, water spraying from her curls. "For this vacation. We're two beautiful women, unencumbered by the demands of the world. Nobody is looking for us. There are no papers to grade, no deadlines to meet, no expectations."

"At least, for this week."

She hugged me. "What more could we ask for?"

"Well, a couple of gorgeous guys would be a nice changeup. Preferably those with jobs and some money to spend on us."

"I suppose you want them to be single as well. Never married. No ex-wives or children to clutter the picture." She flashed me a wicked smile. "Perhaps a virile young monk in training going over the wall."

"A girl can dream, can't she?"

We waded back toward shore. As the sun warmed my shoulders, I thought about her comment. Linda had been seeing a guy named Daniel last month who seemed perfect. Nice looks, a good sense of humor and a decent job. Trouble was he'd lied to her. He claimed to have recently been divorced and was just starting to date again. In reality, he was only separated. Daniel strung his wife along, hinting at the possibility of a reconciliation. And like a fish on the line, she'd take the bait. Whenever he was in the mood for sex, he'd pay his wife a visit. It took Linda just two dates to figure out he wasn't worth her time. She kicked him to the curb and moved on.

We returned to the beach and settled back on the towels, facing the sky. Within minutes, the sun dried us and warmed our skin. I dragged my bag close and used it as a pillow, letting my gaze fall on the lake. It looked like it went on forever. Maybe it did.

After several hours of relaxation and quiet conversation, my stomach grumbled. Loudly. The muffin was a long, distant memory. We gathered up our stuff, pulled on shorts and our cover-ups and walked back into town. I'd noticed one of the restaurants on the main drag served lunch on their rooftop deck. It was busy but we found an umbrella table for four in a corner. From our amazing vantage point, we could see the marina's channel and the lake in the distance.

Linda scanned the menu. I looked over the crowd, scouting to see if there was a popular item being served. Two guys ascended the stairs and searched for seats. Their gazes shifted over the rooftop. One guy was about five foot eight, just a bit taller than me. He had thick blond hair worn a little long. The other guy was shorter and more muscular. Both were wearing slacks and long sleeved dress shirts. Definitely not vacationers. But the rooftop appeared overflowing. I didn't notice any empty tables. They were in for a wait. Linda happened to look up. She sized up the situation in a blink. Pushing her sunglasses on top of her head, she caught the muscular guy's attention and wiggled her fingers at him. I stared at her as he approached.

"Hi." His voice was so deep it belonged in the basement. "I don't mean to impose but I wonder if my friend and I could join you. The place is packed and these are the only seats available. That is, unless you're waiting for someone else."

Linda batted her lashes. "No, it's just the two of us. Please, sit down. Then you can tell us what's good on the menu."

He grinned and motioned to his friend. "I'm Jared. This sorry excuse behind me is Randy." He gently shook our hands and settled into a chair.

Randy followed suit. "I hope it's not an imposition. The food is great. We weren't expecting it to be this busy. Thought the lunch rush would be over by now."

Jared chuckled. "Mr. City Manager there thinks he's still in Milton or whatever you call it in small-town Michigan. I keep telling him this is a vacation town. From Memorial Day to Labor Day, all bets are off. Tourism is big money. It's what makes South Haven a paradise, at least, for a few months every year."

I looked over at the blond. "You're kind of young to be the city manager."

Randy sputtered for a moment, then shrugged. "Yeah, I get that a lot. But I was the deputy manager in Milford—not Milton, Jared— for three years and did a lot of municipal work before then. City planning, downtown development, that kind of thing." He shifted gears quickly. "It's all boring stuff, but necessary. Certainly not the topic of conversation for two lovely ladies on vacation."

"What's the best thing on the menu?" Linda asked, "Because I'm starving."

"The shrimp croissant is excellent," Jared said. "So is the bacon burger with bleu cheese. The fish and chips are better later in the week. And the pulled pork is outstanding. The barbecue sauce has a kick that sneaks up on you."

A young waitress wearing black micro shorts and a tank top with the bar's logo on it appeared. She quickly took our orders. As she wiggled away, I noticed a sparkle on Jared's left hand as he reached for his water glass. A wedding ring. Linda caught it, too. Automatically my eyes went to Randy's hands. No jewelry or the telltale band of pale skin suddenly exposed to sunlight.

"So what do you two do when you're not basking in the sunshine?" Randy asked.

Linda gave them both a sweet smile. "I'm a teacher. High school history. Jamie works for one of the Detroit area major newspapers as an investigative reporter. What about you? Are you really the city manager?"

Randy nodded. "I was hired in February. It's not as big as Milford, nor as close to the metropolitan areas, but important work nonetheless. And, a good career move." He quickly explained some of his duties and responsibilities. I was impressed Linda didn't start yawning. While he filled her in on the busy life of a city planner, I realized he kept his gaze on me, as if memorizing my features. Uncomfortable, I toyed with the straw in my iced tea, then turned to Jared.

"And what keeps you busy?"

Jared barked another deep laugh. "Crime. Nothing as exciting as Detroit, but we still have to uphold the law. Mostly it's keeping the peace, issuing a few traffic tickets, and busting the teenagers sneaking beers. That and chasing after my own kids." He raised his left hand and wiggled his ring finger. "I think you already spotted this."

"That's pretty observant," Linda said with a smile. "How long have you been married?"

There was pride in his voice. "Ten years. High school sweethearts. We got two daughters, six and eight. I did a couple of years at the community college, then went to the police academy. Sara's an RN. She worked in hospitals for a while before signing on with a local doctor. Regular hours let us spend more time as a family."

"Sounds nice," I said. I meant it. It was tough to make a relationship work. "So any big criminal investigations going on?"

Jared raised a hand and grinned. "Oh, you're definitely

a reporter. How about 'no comment'? I'm just here to grab lunch. Which, by the way, Randy is paying for."

We all glanced at him. Randy shrugged. "Tigers beat the White Sox last night. Came from behind late in the seventh."

"You bet against the Tigers?"

He winked at me and grinned. "I thought the Sox were due."

"We can pay for our own lunch," Linda said, using her softest, sultriest voice.

Randy shook his head. "Nah, it's the least we can do, since you were nice enough to share the table. Although, I was going to work the cop here for information."

"We don't want to make the ladies uncomfortable," Jared said.

My reporter's instincts kicked in. I was about to say something when Linda kicked my ankle. Ignoring her, I encouraged Randy to ask his questions. "I promise not to write about it and whatever it is, it won't scare us away."

Randy shrugged. Jared took a pull on his iced tea and reluctantly told us about a complaint he was investigating. Turns out a friend of Randy's vacation home had been broken into and a few things were stolen. Mostly small items, easy to carry. Some liquor as well.

"So, you think it's local kids?"

Jared turned to face me. "What makes you say that?"

I shrugged. "Local kids would know which houses belong to residents and which ones were vacationers. They'd know when the weekend people are gone. So chances are, it could be days or longer before anyone would notice a break-in."

"Do most people with summer cottages come here every weekend?" Linda asked.

Randy responded. "It depends. Some will spend the entire summer up here. Others will come for a week or two, then be gone for a while and return periodically for a weekend."

My curiosity wouldn't be ignored. "Are you sure it's only an isolated incident?"

"What are you getting at?" Jared asked.

"You've got one report. But maybe other places have been hit and the owners are unaware of it. Randy just said a lot of people come and go during the summer."

Before Jared could reply, the food arrived. As we ate, Linda smoothly changed the subject, talking about the various boats we'd seen in the marina.

"Randy's got a boat. I think it's one of the reasons he wanted to move out here," Jared said, pausing to drag a thick French fry through a puddle of ketchup. "He must have dreamed of being Sinbad the Sailor, living onboard his sturdy ship, keeping us safe from marauding pirates. Searching for a mermaid or two."

Randy shrugged. "It keeps me out of trouble."

"I doubt that very much," Linda said with a giggle.

Lunch was a very relaxed meal. The conversation ebbed and flowed over a number of topics, and we never got back to the break-in. As the last of the food was consumed, Jared's phone chimed. He excused himself from the table and took the call. The waitress returned with the check. Despite our efforts, Randy insisted on paying.

"Really, it's my pleasure. We don't often get to share the company of two such lovely ladies. And I enjoyed hearing about things around Motown."

Linda fluttered her fingers at him. "At least, let us return the favor. How about drinks this evening? Maybe around seven?"

Jared returned to the table. "Sorry about that. Got a call from the school. Somebody's been messing around with one of the buses."

"Vandalism?" I asked.

He shook his head and laughed. "Minor league stuff. Mischief. Someone pried open a window and snaked a hose inside, then cranked the faucet on. Janitor found it, but not before the water level was knee deep. Got go check it out." Jared clapped Randy on the shoulder, then waved good-bye.

"He's a good guy. Really gone out of his way to make me feel welcome here." Randy stood. He focused his attention on me. *Did I have something in my teeth?* I ran my tongue over my mouth. How odd.

"So, drinks around seven thirty?" she prompted.

"I know just the place." From a pocket he pulled out a business card. He scrawled something on the back and passed me the card. "See you then. I've got to get back to the office."

Linda reached over and snagged the business card. "Really, it's a wonder you ever get laid, Jamie. That guy was practically drooling over you and you're oblivious."

"Why would he take a second look at me when you're here?"

She flicked a crumb from her plate at me. "His eyes were only on you. I'm surprised he was able to eat his lunch."

There were a couple of times when I noticed his gaze on me, but thought he was trying to be polite. I said as much. She laughed and pushed away from the table.

"You're beautiful, Jamie."

"Next to you, I look like a stick figure."

She put an arm around my shoulders. "You're hopeless. Let's go back to the beach."

CHAPTER TWO

It was a leisurely afternoon. We splashed in the lake and swam for a while, then lounged on the towels in the sunshine. I'd probably tripled the number of freckles on my back and shoulders while Linda got a little more bronze. Taking the long way back to Jake's house, we wandered through a number of quaint little shops. Soon, we were back at the house. Our arms were empty of shopping bags. Just couldn't find anything I needed. Logan was happy to see us, covering our faces with wet kisses. Jake grudgingly accepted a sandy hug, too.

"Dinner's in half an hour. It ain't fancy, but ya won't go hungry."

Linda tried to peer over his shoulder into the kitchen. "What are we having?"

"Dinner. Go rinse off if ya wanna."

We had just enough time for a quick shower. Linda went first while I pulled out some clothes. Jake wisely refused my offers to help in the kitchen. The hot shower tickled my skin. Donning shorts and a tank top, I wandered back outside just as Jake set a platter on the picnic table. Neither Linda nor I knew what to expect.

"It's food," Jake said with a grin. "Grab a plate and

dive in."

Dinner consisted of three New York strip steaks, medium and grilled to perfection. There was a bowl with grilled asparagus and another one with roasted redskin potatoes. Jake had even made a large garden salad with plenty of fresh veggies. I watched as he tossed some bites of steak to the dog. Linda pretended not to notice.

I tasted a little of everything. It was delicious. Turning to the old man, I batted my lashes and clasped my hands together. "Marry me!"

He laughed and took a pull on his beer. "Nah, you're too young for me. Our kids would end up looking like the dog."

"You could always adopt." Linda waved an asparagus spear at him.

"She'd probably want me to change. Like that's gonna happen."

We talked about our day on the beach while Jake shared his day's adventures. Jake and Logan had a relaxing afternoon, with some time at the park along with a stop at the local market. Logan had perfected his fetch routine. Jake napped out in the hammock following several lunchtime beers.

After the meal, Linda and I did the dishes. Jake headed down the street to play cards with some neighbors. To my surprise, Linda hooked the leash on Logan.

"We're taking the dog?"

She bent down and ruffled his coat. "I've barely seen him today. And what better chaperone could you ask for? If Randy doesn't like dogs, he's obviously not worthwhile."

I couldn't argue with her logic.

We walked back to the marina. On the back of his card, Randy had written where his boat was docked. Along the way, we picked up a bottle of wine. The sun was still high in the western sky as we made our way. Linda spotted him. He was wiping down the chrome railings on an older fiberglass speedboat. It was a dark blue, probably about thirty feet long. As we got closer, I could tell it was well cared for.

"Welcome aboard," Randy said, sweeping his right arm wide like a game show host. "It ain't the newest ship in the harbor, but she's all mine." He offered me his left hand. I took it and stepped from the dock.

Logan tugged at the leash and bounded forward. With a laugh, Linda released him and the dog easily jumped to the deck. Randy underwent the canine inspection with a grin, scratching Logan behind the ears with one hand while offering the other to Linda. She took it and gracefully joined us.

There was a large padded bench across the stern. It was about ten feet from there to the cockpit area, where a padded chair was on either side, one by the controls, the other on the passenger side. In front of the bench was a sturdy chrome table, bolted to the floor. A metal ice bucket sat in the center, chilling a bottle of white wine. A stack of plastic cups stood beside it.

Linda settled onto the bench. Logan immediately sprawled at her feet. I moved to a spot alongside her.

"I don't have much in the way of drinks. There's a nice bottle of Chardonnay from a local vineyard. I've got a really smooth Cabernet Sauvignon if you prefer red. Or I can chill the Moscato you brought."

"This sounds good," I said, pointing at the Chardonnay. Linda nodded in agreement.

Randy opened the wine and poured us each a glass. Then he ducked down into the cabin and came back with a large plastic bowl filled with water he set on the deck near Logan. Linda tipped me a wink and a nod. All around us people came and went, walking the pier, boarding different boats or just enjoying the perfect evening. A few boats headed out to the lake. I watched them with a pang of longing.

"Want to go for a cruise?" Randy asked.

Linda flashed a winning smile. "I thought you'd never ask."

Five minutes later, we pulled away from the dock and motored out to Lake Michigan. Linda and the dog remained on the rear bench. I moved up to the cockpit area and watched Randy confidently handle the controls.

Lake Michigan could be deceiving. From a distance, it might look calm and placid. Up close, there's usually some kind of wave action. Of course, the wind and the weather had something to do with it. Tonight, there was very little breeze close to shore and even at eight o'clock, the sun was still bright and high in the western sky. As we exited the marina, Randy turned north and eased down the throttle. He aimed us out, about half a mile from the shoreline and kept watch on any approaching vessels.

I perched on the passenger seat and sat sideways so I could study him. In my peripheral vision, Linda shook her head, her mass of curls streaming behind her. With her arms extended over the back of the seat, she looked like Cleopatra or a royal descendant. I couldn't see her eyes because of the sunglasses, but she was smiling broadly. She flicked her fingers at me and pointed at Randy. Okay, so maybe I don't pick up on signals as quickly as she does. Scooting off the seat, I crossed to the captain's area. The bench here was wide enough for a very fat sailor, or two slender ones.

Randy glanced over as I stood beside him. His left hand dropped from the wheel and tapped the cushion beside him. I leaned against it.

"There's something magical about being out on the lake," he said. I was surprised he didn't have to yell to be heard over the noise from the boat. But with the engine far behind us, we could have a normal conversation.

"Are you out here often?"

"Every chance I get. But the weekends are too crazy. I prefer the weeknights. Or early in the morning, before I go to work."

"Did you have a boat when you were in Milford?"

Randy chuckled and shook his head. "No, I wasn't as close to a big lake. And there was rarely enough time to drive out to Lake St. Clair. That's part of the charm of being in South Haven. The lake is my backyard."

Turned out Randy was living aboard the boat during the summer. He'd bought it in April. After staying in a motel for a few months, he'd moved aboard with the necessities. Down below was a bunk, a small galley and bathroom, with enough storage to meet his needs.

"But what will you do when winter comes?"

He smiled. "Middle or late October, I'll have the boat put into dry-dock. I've already made arrangements. And last month, I met a nice retired couple who have a small house about a mile from the lake. They're snowbirds. Around the same time, they'll head south, visiting friends and family in Florida, Tennessee, Georgia, Texas and New Mexico. While they're gone, I'm going to rent their place. They don't come back until the middle of May. By then, I'll be back on the boat."

"What a great plan."

Randy glanced over his shoulder to check on Linda. "She and Logan look pretty comfortable back there."

I looked back and waved. Linda wiggled her fingers at me. By now, I'd slid up onto the seat beside Randy, close enough so our thighs brushed. Turning back around, I caught him staring at me. Neither of us wore sunglasses.

"Aren't you supposed to be watching for other boats?"

"I can multitask. But no other sailor would blame me for being distracted by such a beautiful woman."

My face warmed. I was about to make a smart-ass comment when he leaned over and kissed me, lightly on the lips. Now, my whole body was blushing.

Randy straightened up and quickly checked the water around us. "Hope I didn't upset you. I've been wanting to do that all night."

"I'm glad you did."

He dropped his left hand from the wheel again and took mine. "Actually, that's not completely true."

"A partial truth?"

"I thought about kissing you at lunch today, but didn't want to scare you off."

Reaching up with my free hand I ran it through his thick blond hair. I stalled, not sure what to say. He watched me closely, shifting his gaze to the water briefly, then coming back to focus on me. "So is this your routine, how you pick up women on vacation?"

"Never done it before. I'm not the Casanova type."

"So you're just drawn to scrawny redheads?"

His hand squeezed mine. "You are not scrawny. You're slender. I've always been attracted to slender women."

His words charmed me. "I'm invisible when Linda's in the vicinity."

That earned me another kiss. This one lasted for about an hour. Well, maybe it was a minute or two. My hand tangled in his hair, keeping him close.

"Glad I'm different from most guys," he said quietly as we separated. His hands returning to the wheel.

Part of me was still locked on his kiss. Was this really happening? I looked back at Linda. She flashed a wide grin and made a show of slowly clapping her hands together. I wondered if she knew how to drive a boat so I could drag Randy to the cabin below deck. With an effort, I reined in such thoughts.

"So I'm supposed to believe you don't find young women out looking for fun on their vacation and charm them with that smile?"

"You like my smile? I always thought it was kind of lopsided."

I took his face in both hands and turned it toward me. "Maybe a little crooked. But that's part of the appeal." Now I initiated a kiss. His hands slid through my hair, then softly ran his fingers down my neck. Shivers of excitement coursed through me. A horn sounded nearby. He broke the kiss and turned to check the water. Another boat passed in the opposite direction. A man and woman were at the helm, mirroring our positions, caught in the moment and sensuality of being on the water. I bit down on my bottom lip in frustration. I longed for more than kisses but safety came first.

"We don't want to run into some sailboat out here," Randy said with a grin.

I scooted back onto the bench. *Maybe a little distance was in order? It might help my racing hormones.* "How fast are we going?"

"About thirty. Want to go faster?"

Was he talking about the boat, or the two of us? Randy shifted. His right hand had dropped to the controls, his left lightly holding the steering wheel. He watched me, his lopsided grin worked its magic. "Shall we give Linda a thrill?"

"I think she's already getting one."

Randy jammed the throttle most of the way down and the boat jumped forward as if launched from a rocket. Linda squealed in delight. I watched the bow come up and bounce a couple of times as the boat adjusted. Even with the additional blast of cool lake air, I still tingled from those kisses.

With the sun beginning to set, Randy steered us into a wide U-turn and headed back toward the marina. Reluctantly, I pushed off the bench and moved back to Linda. Dropping on the seat beside her, I could almost see my reflection in her dazzling smile.

"Thought you said the dog was going to be my chaperone."

She gave me a rolling laugh. "Poor baby had to cover his eyes. He's not used to seeing his aunt get frisky."

"Was I really making out with him, or did I just imagine that?"

"Jamie, you certainly seemed to be enjoying the attention. Why do you find it so hard to believe that a nice looking man would be attracted to you?"

I shrugged. "I'm not blessed with your face and figure, so it's not like guys are fighting over me."

"You are a beautiful woman. Randy certainly seems to think so. Should I take Logan home and leave you two alone?"

We were entering the canal for the marina now. The boat was moving slowly. It made me think of cars exiting the freeway and blending in with traffic on residential streets.

"I'm not ready for anything else tonight."

She smiled and hugged me. "Smart and beautiful. No wonder I love you."

I helped Randy with the lines when we got back to the dock. He walked us through the marina to the main road.

"Thank you for the wine and the ride on the lake," Linda said sweetly. She leaned over and brushed her cheek against his.

"It was my pleasure. Come back any time." He dropped to a knee and rubbed Logan's head. "And that goes for you, too."

Linda led the dog to a patch of grass where he did his business. Somehow Randy had taken my hand when I wasn't looking. "Thanks for a wonderful evening," I said softly.

"Doesn't have to end yet."

I put my free hand on his chest. Through his T-shirt I could feel the steady thump of his heart. *Was it my imagination, or was it beating fast?* "I'm not one to rush things."

"Understood. But I'd really like to see you again."

"Tomorrow night?"

He drew me close. "Dinner. Six o'clock on the boat."

I darted in for a good night kiss. It must have lasted longer than expected because Linda was clearing her throat behind me. People walked around us. There were more than a few smiles in our direction when I found the strength to step back. "Dinner sounds great."

"Good night, Jamie."

"Night."

***

Slowly, we strolled home in the twilight. Logan checked the area, marking his turf as we crossed through the neighborhoods. I tried not to think about Randy. Images of taking him down to the berth below deck and jumping his bones flashed through my mind. Granted, it had been a while since any guy had shown interest in me. But this was moving way too fast. I realized Linda was talking but had no idea what she'd said. Her last comment jolted me back to the present.

"Did you see that kid, Jamie?"

"What kid?"

She laughed and pushed playfully at my shoulder. "Leave Planet Romance for a minute and come back to earth. There was a kid, darting between houses over there. Teenager."

A shake of my head cleared my thoughts. "Could be any number of reasons. It's summer time. Kids are out enjoying the fresh air. Maybe he was just walking home from a friend's house and taking a shortcut."

"Or maybe he's a peeping Tom," she giggled.

"Or an international spy, trying to find the recipe for the perfect margarita."

"Or he's hoping Uncle Jake didn't finish all those beers in that old washtub and left some out for an adventurous lad."

I noticed about half the houses on the street were dark. Probably belonged to summer people. Not everyone could afford the properties that offered a view of the lake. Many of these homes would be ideal for a family vacation. Depending on their proximity to South Haven, they could see frequent use. Reluctantly, I pushed thoughts of Randy to the back of my mind.

"We should go exploring tomorrow, Linda."

"One day in the sand and you're already bored?"

"Hardly. But I've never been here before. I noticed on the main drag a shop which rented bicycles and scooters. There's a lot more to see than just the marina and the beach. We could cruise around in the morning, then hit the beach in the afternoon."

Logan guided us into the driveway at Jake's house. "It does sound like fun. But that means we need to get moving early. No lounging in bed until noon," Linda said.

"That's fine with me."

Jake was still at his neighbors. We sat for a few minutes in the screened in porch. Darkness had taken over. The stars had begun to show. If you listened closely, you heard the sound of the waves and above that, the light buzz of mosquitos as they came out to play. We sprawled at opposite ends of a rattan sofa as we enjoyed the night air. Linda adjusted the thick cushion beneath her and lightly kicked my leg.

"He's a nice guy. Good looking, too."

I smiled. No argument from me. "Yeah."

"You seemed to enjoy his attention."

"Yeah."

"Smooth moves, too. Those kisses were getting pretty intense."

"Yeah."

She smacked me with a pillow. "There's no reason in the world you shouldn't have some fun. We're only here for the week. Enjoy it."

"It just surprised me. I wasn't expecting to meet anybody."

"That's the beauty of it. Your magnetic charms drew him in at lunchtime. Poor guy never had a chance."

I laughed. "My magnetic charms?"

"I've known you since the first grade. Some guys take one look at you and fall under your spell. Those inquisitive green eyes. The dark red hair. One good look and they never have a chance. They're magnetically drawn in. You just don't realize it."

"From now on, you'd better point those guys out. I must have been missing the signals." I bit back a yawn and threw my pillow at her. "Time for bed."

CHAPTER THREE

Tuesday morning was another picture perfect day. At the rental place, we opted for small scooters. Together, we zoomed around the area, drove beyond the marina, and explored the northern part of the city, where a number of million-dollar homes faced the water. Some looked like palaces, others more laid back. We discovered rows of shops and even more white sandy beaches. Dressed in tank tops and shorts, we garnered more than a few waves from people as we cruised along.

We stopped at a coffee bar for a jolt of caffeine. Linda was examining the menu board when a deep voice sounded behind me.

"Think I'll let you two off with a warning this time. There has been half a dozen near-miss accidents caused by guys watching you instead of the road."

I turned around, laughing. "Some things are beyond our control, officer."

Jared chuckled. "Actually, it's sergeant. Having a good time?"

"The best. How bad was the school bus?"

He waved a stubby finger at me. "Almost forgot you're a reporter."

Linda pushed playfully at my shoulder. “She does not have a tape recorder or note pad tucked into her clothing. But I’d understand if you had to search her, just to be certain.”

He chuckled again and threw a broad wink at her. “Why do I get the feeling you expect me to search her?”

“Well, if you’re reluctant to do it, perhaps you could recommend someone who would. In the name of public safety and all.”

I felt the flush of embarrassment start at my toes and rocket through my body. Subtlety was not her style. I gestured at the menu board. “So what do you recommend?”

“I’m an old fashioned guy. Just coffee. But I take mine with a short blast of caramel. My daughters got me hooked on it.” Jared grinned. I was happy to move on to safer ground and avoid Linda’s hints at searching me.

Coffees in hand, we walked outside to one of the patio tables with Jared taking a chair where he could watch the traffic going by, both vehicular and pedestrian. Maybe cops were always on alert. Linda and Jared were chatting about the area. I let me guard down for a minute and relaxed, soaked up the sunshine.

“Bumped into Randy this morning by the office. Said he had a great time on the lake last night.” Jared’s eyes bored into me. I choked on my coffee.

Linda nodded sweetly. “Yes, it was a great time. Don’t you agree, Jamie?”

“Absolutely.” The warmth had returned in full force.

Jared’s phone beeped. He apologized, then checked a text message. “Gotta run. Hey, if you’re in town Wednesday night, there’s a great band concert in the park. Starts about 7:00. Lots of good music.”

“We’ll check it out,” Linda said.

Jared saluted with his coffee cup. “Have fun. Maybe we’ll bump into each other again.”

“I wouldn’t be a bit surprised.”

We watched him move quickly to an older sedan and drive away. Linda had a devilish expression on her face.

"You do realize you were as red as your hair. And, don't tell me its sunburn."

"No, it's windburn. From riding around on the scooters."

She shook her head. "Jamie, you are so full of shit."

"I can't believe you were encouraging him to frisk me. And suggesting someone else should do it!"

"He'd already talked to Randy. Maybe, he mentioned getting to second base last night."

I wanted to smack her. "He did not. Randy was a perfect gentleman."

"Well, you got the perfect part right," she said with a laugh.

***

After dropping the scooters off, we opted for salads at a small café. It was early afternoon when we found a nice spot on the beach. We went for a swim, reveling in the lake. Back on the sand, sprawled on our towels, I dozed off. The warmth of the sun, the gentle sound of the waves breaking on the shore and the overall sense of relaxation combined to lull me to sleep. Later we went for another swim, going parallel to our spot on the beach for a hundred yards or more, then swimming back and forth twice more. I was wide-awake from all the exercise. My muscles tingled from the cold lake water. We packed up and leisurely walked home.

"Don't be nervous," Linda said as we neared the house.

"I wasn't until you said it."

"Relax and be yourself. That's who Randy is interested in."

"What are you going to do tonight?"

Linda smiled and shook back her hair. "I'm going to spend a relaxing evening with Jake and Logan. Maybe read a little. Watch the stars come out. Nothing stressful."

"Sounds nice." My voice sounded a little jittery.

She linked her arm through mine. "Breathe. Just breathe."

"I'll try."

Linda offered to drive me to the marina but I opted to walk. The stroll gave me a chance to mingle with the other vacationers who wandered the streets of this beautiful little city. After two days in the sunshine, I was more than a little pink. Not expecting to go on a date, I hadn't packed anything other than shorts and tops. I was wearing a pair of navy-blue shorts and a sleeveless white blouse. Tennis shoes completed my ensemble.

Randy stood on the dock and watched me approach. I sensed he'd been waiting for a little bit. Maybe he had been checking out the other women walking by. But his gaze remained fixed on me as I drew closer.

"Hi," I said nervously.

"Hey." He reached out and took my hand. As he slowly pulled me closer, he turned me around, like a spin on the dance floor. Fortunately, I didn't stumble over my own feet. The next thing I knew, he was kissing me. Or maybe I was kissing him. Did it matter who started it?

Reluctantly, we separated. Randy guided me aboard. On the little table at the stern were dishes, silverware, napkins and two carryout containers. There was a bottle of red wine and two plastic cups.

"I promised you dinner."

"What are we having?"

"Chinese. Beef with broccoli or shrimp with snow peas." He flashed me his crooked smile and shrugged. "I'm not much of a cook."

"Neither am I."

We settled on the couch and dug into the food, sharing both entrees. The wine was very smooth. During the meal, the conversation was light, little bits about the day, the area and some spots in metro Detroit we were both familiar with. Randy got up to clean up the food containers then returned.

"Linda and I enjoyed seeing more of the town. Oh I almost forgot, we ran into Jared earlier today."

Randy's grin widened. "I heard something about that."

"Oh shit."

"The police station is in the same building as the city offices. It's not uncommon for Jared and me to cross paths several times during the day. So late this afternoon he told me about the coffee bar. And Linda's comments about searching you."

My reaction surprised me. Maybe it was the wine. Or the combination of the fresh air, the gently rocking boat and the handsome guy sitting close to me. But instead of blushing, I leaned in and kissed him, very lightly.

"Want to search me?" I whispered.

"Oh yeah."

Randy got to his feet and took my hand. He led me to the cabin. Once we were down below, he turned and slid the overhead hatch in place and closed the door. Hopefully, it would keep away any prying eyes.

I trembled with anticipation. It had been a while since my last romantic overture. When Randy drew me to him, I couldn't tell if it was me shaking or the boat rocking. Somehow, I managed to get my arms around his neck. When he kissed me, my instincts kicked in. Our clothes were slowly removed until we were standing there, naked, pressed tightly together.

The bunk was wide and comfortable, although I wouldn't have noticed if we were on burlap or sandpaper. My focus was on Randy as his was on me. Together, we added our own efforts to keep the boat rocking. Afterward, we lay curled on our sides, facing each other, and catching our breath. Our fingers gently caressed, seeking each other out.

"Did you discover anything while searching me?"

He flashed his crooked smile. "Jared would remind me

to be thorough. You never know what I might find hidden somewhere." His hand slid down my back and cupped my ass, drawing me even closer.

I reached back and slapped his hand. "Trust me, there is nothing hidden back there."

"Well, maybe I should check this side." His hands slid over my skin, touching some very sensitive areas. My fingers were busy as well.

"You gonna search me again?"

"Oh yeah."

***

It was almost sunset. We were out on the lake, enjoying the cool air, and guiding the boat north, about half a mile from the shore. The moon was rising. I had reclaimed my bra and panties. I felt decadent wearing only my underwear, but out on the lake, no one could really see me. Randy was wearing a pair of shorts. He sat in the captain's chair, legs dangling while I stood in front of him, and held the steering wheel with both hands. I finally was driving his boat. The feel of the wheel between my hands and the soft sway of the boat under my feet was exhilarating. Another check mark off my bucket list. When he leaned forward and nuzzled my neck, a gasp of surprise escaped me. He moved from holding my waist to keep me steady to running his hands up and down my meager curves, sending shivers through my body.

"Still searching me?"

"No, just enjoying the warmth of you."

I let go of the wheel and spun around to face him. There was still enough light to see his features clearly. One kiss led to another. Thankfully, there were no boats within a mile of us. If there was a club like the "Mile High Club", we became members. Soon, Randy reclaimed the wheel and his shorts and steered us back to the marina. At the dock, I went below and quickly dressed.

"You could stay the night."

I shook my head, sending my red locks dancing. "Thanks, but I'd rather go home. Besides, you'll need to get some sleep before work in the morning."

"I could sleep with you in my arms." Randy drew me close.

"That's cute."

"At least, let me drive you."

I shrugged. "What the hell. Okay, but don't expect to be making out in the driveway. Linda will probably be spying out the windows."

"All right."

We locked up the boat and strolled to the marina's parking lot. Randy had a medium size SUV, something that was probably a requirement in the winter, considering how much snow blasted the area around the lake. With the windows down, the night air felt invigorating. Or maybe it was the result of multiple rounds of sex. Randy followed my directions as we moved slowly through the residential streets.

"What was that?"

He turned toward me. "What was what?"

"Over there, by that house with the blue trim. Something ran across the yard."

"Probably a dog."

"You grow dogs that are six feet tall over here?"

Randy stopped. After checking his mirror, he put the truck in reverse and rolled backward. When we were in front of the house in question, he swung into the driveway. The place was dark. There was no evidence anyone was home. Probably a vacation home, like so many others in the area.

"I still don't see anything," Randy said.

"Got a flashlight?"

"Seriously? You want to check out a stranger's house?"

"Yep."

He dug a small flashlight out of the center console.

Randy shut down the truck and left the headlights on. Together we got out and walked up the driveway. I sensed he was just humoring me. When he stopped, I took the light and kept moving. Randy followed. The grass in the yard was thick, as if it hadn't been cut in a couple of weeks. You could see footprints in it, running across the yard diagonally. I motioned my find to him.

"Probably kids, taking a shortcut to get home before curfew."

"You really think so?" I asked.

"Yeah. Look, they don't even go close to the building." Randy's arm was around my waist now, drawing me in. If he was trying to distract me with his physicality, he was doing a damn fine job of it. I gave up and let him turn me around. We stopped alongside the truck and shared a few more kisses.

"Neighbors will complain if we don't move along," I whispered in his ear.

"They might be enjoying the show. Or getting inspired."

His comment had me smiling. "Let them write their own ending." I pushed him away and climbed back into the truck.

***

It didn't surprise me to find Linda on the screened in porch, curled up on one end of the rattan sofa. Logan was sprawled by her feet. The loyal dog always stayed close when she was around. There was one lamp on behind her, throwing just enough light to read by. She was in the middle of the latest John Sandford mystery. Linda glanced up, a gentle smile on her face.

"You're glowing."

I waved the comment aside and sank to the cushions on the opposite end of the sofa. "It was a lovely evening."

"I want details."

"Go away!"

She shook her head, the smile growing wider. "Details. Was there wine? Dinner? Dancing? And then romancing? Or did you skip the preliminaries and foreplay and just shred each other's clothes?"

"Seriously? You think I'll tell you everything?"

"You know you will. Besides, you smell a little sweaty, your blouse isn't buttoned right and you have this very pleased expression on your face. So, yes, I believe you had sex. And you're going to tell me all about it."

Stifling my laughter so we wouldn't wake up Jake, I told her about the evening. *Hey, she's my best friend. We knew everything about each other. There were no secrets.*

"Are you going to see him again?"

We hadn't talked about it but I sensed it would happen. This had turned out to be a great vacation so far. The fact I'd connected with a guy before she did was still a bit of a surprise. I mentioned the detour we made, which turned out to be just two blocks away. Linda shook her head, her eyes twinkling in the soft light.

"Jamie, only you would go looking for a story instead of paying attention to the guy beside you."

"I wasn't looking for a story. I just noticed something odd."

"Want to do some more exploring in the morning?"

"Sure. Think I'll go take a shower and head off to bed."

She sniffed and pulled her head back a little. "A shower would be a good idea."

I threw a pillow at her and left the room.

CHAPTER FOUR

Wednesday morning, we dressed for the beach. It was another picture perfect day. I was beginning to think clouds were not allowed in South Haven during the summer. Maybe the Chamber of Commerce controlled the weather. As we walked along, I stopped in front of the house with the blue trim. Linda reluctantly followed as I went up the driveway.

"Jamie, what are we doing?"

"I'm curious. That's two nights in a row where we've seen someone running in the dark. Maybe there is something going on."

"Why are you looking for trouble? We're on vacation. Is this a way of diverting my attention from your misbehavior?" A wicked grin flashed across her face.

Ignoring her, I stood at the back of the house. The footprints were still visible in the yard. Randy had been right. There were no signs of activity near the building. But if they were running away from here, where did they come from? I turned around and faced the street, following the diagonal path. I could imagine someone racing between the two houses on the opposite side of the road. Curiosity got the better of me. We walked in that direction. Both houses were dark with no signs of life. I went between them to the backyards.

"Jamie, let's go. The beach is waiting. Sun, sand, muscular lifeguards with tiny swimsuits could be looking for us even as we're standing here."

"There are no lifeguards on our part of the beach."

"Maybe they're on vacation, too."

I was about to give up when something caught my eye. The back door to the house on the left, a quaint little cottage, was pried open. There were several gouges in the wood. Peeking through the window, I could see into the kitchen. The cupboard doors were ajar. Linda stood silently beside me for a moment. Then she moved around the corner. She returned, shaking her head in dismay.

"There's a gap in the curtains on the side window. The place looks ransacked." From her straw bag, she dug out her cell phone and a small piece of paper. I realized it was Randy's business card from the other day. We walked down the driveway so we could find an address number. The look she gave me was less than friendly. "Only you, Jamie. Only you."

Five minutes later, a police car pulled up in front. The uniformed officer had just begun taking down our information when another vehicle parked behind him. Jared stepped out of the car, drumming his fingers on the roof. But there were traces of a grin on his face.

"We gotta stop meeting like this. My wife is gonna get suspicious."

"It's not me," Linda said innocently. "It's her."

He walked up the driveway. "Let's hear how you two just happened to stumble onto this. Because it seems like the last thing you'd be doing on a vacation."

Linda hesitated. "You'd better tell it from last night, Jamie. But maybe leave out all the hot and sweaty parts."

"I'll only give you the details that are pertinent."

Jared was chuckling. "Yeah, I bumped into Randy this morning. I think he'll be worthless most of the day. Did he search you?"

"I refuse to answer on the grounds that it's none of your business. Do you want to hear about finding this house or not?"

"Yes, let's have it."

So I spelled it out for him. Together, we walked across to the house with the blue trim. Jared checked the backyard, where the footprints were mostly gone. We went back across the street. The other cop was waiting by the patrol car.

"Dispatch ran the address. The owners live in Jackson. They try to come out every other weekend. County Sherriff is sending their forensic people, but it will be awhile before they get here. How do you want to handle it?"

Jared considered it for a moment. An idea jumped to the front of my brain and I blurted it without thinking.

"If you have video on your phone, you could go inside and film how the house looks. Then send it to the owners and see if they can identify anything missing."

"That's a good idea. We'll wait for forensic to do their thing," Jared said. He glanced at Linda. "No need for you two to stick around. Go enjoy the beach."

"We'll leave it to you." She grabbed my arm and steered me away. "This is turning out to be a strange vacation."

"Are you kidding? It's gotta be the best vacation ever!"

"You really do need to get laid more often."

***

It was after one. We'd been swimming and tanning for a while and were lounging on the towels talking about little things, when the phone in Linda's bag chimed. She dug it out and responded with a series of one-word answers. Then she broke the connection, stowed the phone and rolled to her knees.

"What's going on?"

"Free lunch with a handsome man." Linda dug her shorts out and wiggled them on. Then she gathered up the rest of her belongings and jammed them into the bag. "What are you waiting for?"

"A little more information would be nice."

"We can talk on the way. Move your ass, Jamie. We might even get a glass of wine."

I sensed she wouldn't tell me more until we were in motion. Quickly, I grabbed my gear and followed her across the sand. All I got was more one-word answers until we were into the town. Linda stopped at a corner and brushed sand from her arms and legs. She turned around and I cleared her back and bottom. Smiling sweetly, she faced me and returned the favor. Done with the sand, she slapped my butt.

"We're going to Clementine's."

"I thought you said it was expensive."

"It is but it's a great place when someone else is buying."

The restaurant was on the opposite corner. Even well past lunchtime, there were people lined up on the sidewalk, waiting for a table. Linda smiled and sashayed through the crowd. I followed, more curious than ever. She whispered something to the hostess and was immediately led into the dining room. *What was going on?*

Sitting at a large round table with his back to the wall was Jared. A petite dark haired woman was at his side. She looked us up and down before facing him. "Yes, I can see what you mean. Poor Randy never had a chance."

"This is my wife, Sara."

"The nurse," Linda said.

She beamed a smile. "That's right. Jared was just telling me about your morning discovery. Kind of unusual for South Haven."

"Did you learn what was missing?" I asked.

His eyes flicked to Sara. "Reporter."

"Investigative reporter," I corrected with a grin. "So, whatcha find out?"

"The list consisted of--two computers, a video game console, about a dozen game cartridges, over three hundred bucks in cash and a few bottles of booze."

I took a moment to consider the information while Sara encouraged us to sit down. "So you're looking for at least two people. Probably a van or an SUV. Something that wouldn't raise any suspicions in the neighborhood at night."

"How did you make that jump?" Jared asked.

"Easy. The kid we saw was running. There's no way he could carry all the stuff."

Sara watched our exchange like a tennis match. "Is she right?"

"Probably. One of the neighbors had a sprinkler system going last night. We found a lot of footprints running in the opposite direction. Diagonal. So we're thinking it's a couple of kids who break in, do a grab and go, loading their haul into some type of car and taking off."

"The loot sounds like something kids would go after. Video games and liquor. Was there anything else of value?" Linda asked.

Jared's eyes traced back and forth between us. I noticed he was slowly tapping a finger on the table, as if deciding what to do. Sara reached over and placed a hand over his. "Tell them. What can it hurt?"

He glanced at his wife then curled his hand around hers. "You're right. There were also some paintings stolen. The owner says they were worth a lot, maybe a couple of grand. Not the usual beach stuff, but from a gallery in Saugatuck. That's an artist community. There was also a small sculpture missing."

"Kids aren't going to bother with art. There's someone behind this who knows valuables. Somebody working with the kids," I said.

"Yeah, it looks like South Haven has its very own

Fagan," Sara said.

The waitress appeared. We ordered quickly. I noticed Linda opted for iced tea instead of wine. I did the same. Sara shifted the conversation away from crime, asking about our plans and how long we'd be in the area.

"You've got to come to the park for the concert tonight. Music begins right at 7:00. You'll like the band. They play a lot of classic rock covers. Good variety."

"Do they draw a big crowd?" Linda asked.

Sara grinned. "Absolutely. A lot of people will bring camp chairs or blankets. There are a couple of food trucks there, too. It's a lot of fun."

"We'll check it out."

Sara proved to be a masterful hostess. She kept the conversation flowing and steered us away from any discussion of the robbery. It may have been my imagination, but I thought she wiggled her chair a bit closer to Jared. Linda attempted twice to pay for our meals, but Jared waved it away.

"Come to the park tonight. You will definitely enjoy it," he said.

"We'll be there," I said.

Outside we watched the happy couple walk away. Linda twirled her straw bag, spinning the handles one way, then the other. I could tell there was something on her mind. After all these years, I knew she'd talk when she was ready.

"Back to the beach, or should we prowl through some of these lovely stores?"

"Shopping sounds like a nice diversion."

***

That evening the four of us walked to the park for the concert. Linda had called Jake earlier and told him not to cook. Logan led the way. As we got close, Linda winked at me and hooked her arm through Jake's right arm. I copied her move on the other side. The old guy stopped walking. He looked me up and down, then did the same with Linda. Nodding his assent, we continued into the park. Jake acknowledged a few neighbors and friends as we passed, acting as if being accompanied by a pair young women was an everyday occurrence.

"You're a lecherous old man," Linda teased.

"You started it. Now I'll be eating free meals for a month from all the widows who want to take your place. They must believe the old saying."

"What old saying?" I asked.

He gave me a comical grin. "Once you go gray, you won't ever stray!"

We located a good spot on the grass to the left of the bandstand. Each of us carried a camp chair that was easy to set up. Logan curled up in the grass at Linda's feet. Jake and I went to scope out the food trucks. There was a barbecue truck called Bomba's, with pulled pork sandwiches and half slabs of ribs, a taco truck, another with ice cream and fresh lemonade and one serving fried chicken and potatoes. It was a good thing we'd had salads for lunch. I texted Linda the options. We both went for pulled pork. Jake couldn't make up his mind, so he got both ribs and chicken. Together, we carried all the food back to our spot.

Shortly after we finished eating, the band warmed up. People milled around, enjoying the beautiful summer evening. There was a good breeze coming in from the lake which kept the bugs away. Jake strolled over to chat with some old fishing buddies. I scanned the crowd. Subconsciously, I must have been searching for Randy. *Why hadn't he called me? He didn't strike me as the one-night stand kind of guy. But what did I know? My track record when it came to dating wasn't something that would make headlines.*

"Jamie, are you listening to me?"

"Sorry, my mind was drifting."

"I said you should check out the band."

On the bandstand were three guys and a woman. I stared in disbelief. The woman was Sara. She stepped behind the microphone and adjusted the strap for an acoustic guitar. There was a younger kid behind the drums, maybe no more than sixteen. An older guy with long silver hair pulled into a ponytail limbered up on the saxophone. The last guy was running through the scales on an electronic keyboard. His blond hair drew me in. He looked up and our eyes met. A crooked smile crossed his face. He raised his shoulders in a bashful shrug.

"What the hell. Did you know about this?"

Linda smiled sweetly. "Of course. I'm a teacher. I know everything."

Once they started playing, I was mesmerized. For the next hour the band went through a variety of songs, from big band tunes of the 40's to some current hits. Sara played well and had an excellent voice. Randy and the drummer pitched in with background vocals. While he was mainly focused on the songs, swaying back and forth behind the keyboard, he snuck glances at me as much as possible.

I was on my feet like many others, moving to the music. Jared appeared beside me with two plastic cups of lemonade. He winked as he handed one over.

"How do you like them?"

"They're amazing. Why didn't you tell me who was in the band?"

"And spoil the surprise? Not a chance."

I grinned and curled my fingers at him, urging him to dance with me. Jared took our drinks and set them beneath my chair. In a very fluid move, he caught my hand and spun me around. For a stocky guy, he was very light on his feet. We danced together for a couple of numbers. Linda and Jake had been slow dancing as well. As the song ended, Sara announced they were going to take a quick break.

"How long have they been performing together?"

Jared considered it. "Randy started here in February.

One of the bars had an open mic night on Saturdays. He heard Sara sing. There was an old piano in the corner. He started to accompany her. One thing led to another."

Sara appeared beside him. She swiped his lemonade and chugged it. "Having fun?"

"Absolutely."

Randy stood sheepishly behind her. "Hi, Jamie. Want to get something to drink?"

I pushed my cup at Linda. "Sure."

There was polite laughter behind us, but I didn't care. He took my hand as we walked toward the trucks. I was tempted to pull him behind a tree and have my way with him, but there were too many people around. Even some children. Still it was tempting.

"You play well. Nice job on the vocals, too."

His crooked smile went up a little. "Thanks. Gotta stay within my range. I'm okay with background stuff, but that's about it."

"Do you have any other hidden talents you're keeping secret?"

Randy leaned in for a kiss. "Time will tell."

***

It was late when the concert ended. Linda, Jake and Logan headed home. Jared and I helped Sara and the others pack their gear up. Randy eyes were full of questions as we loaded the keyboard and stand in the back of the SUV.

"Wanna walk me home?"

"Sure."

He took my camp chair and slung the strap over his shoulder. We waved good-bye to the others. It was surprising how quickly the area around the park had grown quiet. Only a handful of people were still on the streets, strolling along. Above us, the stars had started to come out. Neither one of us spoke, but the silence was comfortable. At one corner, Randy stopped walking and pulled me closer. He kissed me. My heart raced. He had one hand on my ass, the other cupping the back of my head. My arms were around his neck.

Gasping with desire, I broke the kiss. Pushing him away, I turned around to get my bearings. Randy's hands were on my waist, keeping me steady.

"It's late," I whispered to the darkness.

"Not that late."

"They'll be waiting for me."

I let him draw me close again, feeling his chest against my back. My eyes searched the darkness. Then I saw it. With an effort, I took a step away.

"We have to hurry."

"What's the rush?" his voice was raspy. From too much singing or too much arousal, I couldn't say for sure. It didn't matter.

Grabbing his arm, I led him across the road. There was an old barn at the back of the lot. Large trees provided a barrier behind it. We were hidden from any prying eyes. I stopped in the shadows and faced him.

"Set up the chair."

Randy didn't understand. He reached for me and I pushed his hand away.

"Set up the chair. Take off your pants and sit down."

"Are you serious?"

I was already undoing my shorts. "It's a quickie or nothing."

"I'll take the quickie."

"Then set up the damn chair. I am *not* rolling around in the grass."

It's amazing what you can accomplish with the proper motivation.

***

Linda sat up in bed reading. Logan lay curled in the

corner. He raised his head briefly as I entered the room, then relaxed. She was having a difficult time keeping a straight face. I recalled seeing her dance with a number of men during the concert. That same expression appeared on more than one occasion when a guy would get a little too friendly. It bordered on innocence. She gave up and beamed a smile at me.

"Did you take the long way home?"

I flopped on the bed beside her. "Shut up."

"You're very flushed."

"It's a warm night."

"Not that warm. Actually there's a lovely cool breeze coming off the lake. And speaking of coming…"

"Shut up," I said playfully. She closed her book and slid down alongside me.

'I'm happy for you. Randy is a really nice guy. The way he lights up around you is special."

"He is pretty cool." I dragged a finger down her bronzed arm. It was still difficult to believe what had happened these last few nights. At some point, I expected to awaken and discover it was all a lovely dream.

"We're only here for a few more days. Or do you think this could lead to something else? It's a four-hour drive from home."

I gave my head a slow shake. "Don't think I could handle a long distance relationship. We're just having fun."

"A lot of fun."

"Yeah."

She couldn't stop smiling at me. "A lot of earth shattering, hot and steamy, passionate fun. At least, there aren't any grass stains on your shorts."

"Shut up."

"Go shower."

CHAPTER FIVE

Thursday morning, we stopped for fried egg sandwiches and coffee on our way to the beach. Jake and Logan were headed to a farmer's market to stock up on goodies. Jake had discovered Logan was a babe magnet. I got the feeling Jake might get a pup of his own when we left on Sunday. As we walked through the town, I pulled up short in front of an office.

"What's going on?" Linda asked.

"My mind is stuck. I need something to distract me."

"From the hot and sweaty sex?"

"Hush. Just follow my lead."

I walked into the real estate office. Inside were pictures of numerous houses for sale. Some were quaint little cottages. Others were massive. And everything in between. A lady named Cynthia came forward and offered to help.

"I'm wondering if there are any people who rent out their vacation homes," I said.

"Of course. We have quite a few who are willing to do that. Many of them use our offices to screen clients. I'd be happy to show you some properties."

Over Cynthia's shoulder I saw Linda roll her eyes. This was the last thing she wanted to do this morning. I persuaded Cynthia to give me a map of the area and a number of data sheets about the rental properties. She also gave me pages on a couple of units that were for sale. Jamming the papers into my straw bag, we went to our favorite spot on the beach.

Linda stripped off her shorts and cover up. She threw them at me as I anchored my towel on the sand. "What are you up to?"

"Nothing. Just curious about the area. It's so nice here." I took the bottle of sunscreen from her and began to cover her back and shoulders.

"Bullshit, Jamie. I've known you forever. And I can hear the gears turning on your brain. You're up to something. And it's not late night skinny dipping off Randy's boat."

"That's a great idea!"

She grabbed the bottle and squirted lotion on my shoulder. "Start talking."

During yesterday morning's adventure, the uniformed officer casually mentioned the address of the earlier break in. It got me thinking about a pattern. The map was laid out on the towel. Linda dug a pencil from her bag. We circled the two locations. According to the information from the real estate office, there were four other houses nearby available for rent or sale. Which meant they were probably unoccupied right now.

"You're not going to let this go," she said with disgust.

"I'm just curious. What can it hurt?"

"With you, that's hard to say."

I called Cynthia. We made arrangements to go see the four houses later this afternoon. Now that I had a plan, I could relax. Stretching out on the towels, we talked about the concert.

"There were several good looking men hanging around you," I said. "Nobody caught your eye?"

She was on her back, arms relaxed at her side. It was almost as if I could hear her skin toasting in the sunshine.

"Nope. I didn't come on this trip looking for romance. And I'm not interested in some one-night-stand with an aspiring lawyer from Chicago."

"I never expected to meet a guy."

"Sometimes, it just happens. Don't get me wrong, I'm glad you and Randy connected. Besides, it's fun to tease you."

"Glad my romantic activities have been the source of your entertainment."

"You deserve to have some fun, Jamie. Randy certainly enjoys your company. But, I wish you'd leave the investigating to the cops."

"Figuring out what's going on with those robberies is fun."

She got up and threw a handful of sand at my stomach before heading for the lake. "You are very weird."

"But that's why you love me." I chased after her.

"Sad, but true."

***

Cynthia was ready when we got back to the office. We started with the one closest to the scene of yesterday's home invasion. It was more of a home than a cottage, with three large bedrooms, a combination great room and kitchen and a big screened in porch. There was no sign of anything out of order. The second house was a little farther away. This was more of a quaint little cottage. Nothing was disturbed, but it didn't look like there was much of value there. Cynthia chatted away as we pulled up to house number three. Suddenly, my nerves tingled. Was this how Spider Gwen felt?

Each house had a realtor's lock box on the front door, where a key was kept. As we started up the driveway, I stepped behind Cynthia and caught Linda's eye. Reluctantly she began talking about the landscaping. Linda led her away from the door. I dashed into the backyard. At first, the house just looked empty and dark. But when I got to the rear door, I saw the pry marks on the wooden frame. Standing on my tiptoes, I could see in the kitchen window. The place was trashed. I ran around front before they got to the door.

"Call Jared."

Linda dug in her purse. Confusion clouded Cynthia's face. Gently I guided her back to the car and explained what was going on. Linda joined us a moment later.

"Jared said, and I'm quoting here, 'stay out of the damn house'."

"I didn't go in. Just saw the door and peeked in the window."

Less than ten minutes later, Jared arrived. A patrol car followed. Jared marched up the driveway and stood glaring at us for a moment. He knew Cynthia. After confirming her role in the discovery, Jared sent her on her way. He looked at me and shook his head in disgust. But I could see the corners of his mouth lifting in a smile.

"Tell me what you figured out."

Spreading the map on the hood of his car, I laid it out for him. Linda joined in, describing the two other homes we visited. She also pointed out the next one on our list. All three properties that had been hit were within a mile of each other. Easy to cover on a bike or on foot. Jared sent the patrol car over to check the last place.

"Going to the real estate office was a good idea," he said reluctantly. "Got any others you'd like to share?"

Linda shook her head, the mass of dark curls swayed in the breeze. Jared glanced at me.

"All the break-ins were on the south side of the marina. From what we saw the other day, the north side has some very extravagant places. Has there been any action over there?"

"Not that we've heard about. The majority of the folks with cottages to the north will be there all summer long. Still, it's worth checking out."

Jared called the station. He sent another patrol unit to the real estate office to pick up a list of rental and sale properties from the north side. From there they would go inspect each unit for any signs of trouble. He had parked beneath a tree, so the car was comfortable in the shade. Linda and I sat on the hood, legs dangling off the side. Jared waited for the county's forensic crew to arrive.

"Know what troubles me?" I asked.

"It's certainly not a lack of pheromones," Linda muttered.

Jared scrubbed his face with his palms. "Okay, I'll bite. What troubles you?"

"What are they doing with the merchandise? Even if it is kids, they've got to stash it somewhere. The booze they'll drink, but what about the other items. And the artwork doesn't fit in. Teenagers are not going to grab paintings or sculptures."

"Unless the paintings were of naked teenage girls," Linda said.

Jared's eyed her quizzically. "Oh yeah. High school teacher. So what do you think?"

"I'm thinking someone's garage or storage unit. Are there any nearby that can be rented? I didn't notice anything when we were driving into town, but wasn't really looking for one."

"There are several places, mostly on the outskirts of the city. Some vacationers will keep their boats or wave runners there. Or other equipment. We can talk to the owners but without probable cause, I can't get a warrant."

I drummed my fingers on the hood. Linda poked me in the ribs. We were interrupted as the crime scene van arrived. Jared held up a palm, indicating he wasn't done with us yet. So we sat in the shade and waited.

"Is this part of some merit badge you never got as a kid?" Linda asked. "If you keep this up, maybe they'll make you a junior detective."

"It's a mystery. I just want to figure it out."

"We could be basking in the sun."

I pointed to the front lawn, which was flooded in bright sunshine. "Bask away."

Half an hour later, Jared was back. "Looks like a bigger score. A couple of flat screen televisions, more booze and two more paintings were taken. The owners said there was also a small wooden box, with intricate carvings on it, that's kind of a family heirloom. The wife kept her jewelry in it. A couple of nice diamonds and a pair of emerald earrings. They didn't break anything, just like the last place. Drawers and cupboards were open, closets gone through. This wasn't a five-minute job. These guys took their time."

"So we need to figure out how they're hauling all this away and what they're doing with the goodies," I said.

It took me a moment to realize Jared was smiling. Not a broad grin, but something that might build up to it. He stared beyond us at a house across the street.

"What's up, Columbo?"

The grin went up another notch. "The owners tell me the house across the street is owned by a friendly guy from Lansing. The friendly guy owns a security business. He's forever upgrading his system. Last summer he installed some cameras around the outside of the house as well. High definition stuff."

"And the cameras?" Linda asked.

"Just so happen to cover the front of this property."

I looked over my shoulder at the other house. "So you can see what kind of vehicle was used. And maybe get a plate."

"Got it in one," Jared said.

Not only did the neighbor have video cameras, the system was always on. He could also access it remotely. Jared took a call a few minutes later. The guy had checked the files. The homeowners had been there the previous weekend. On Monday night at eleven-fifty-five, a dark blue or black van pulled into the driveway. It went all the way to the rear of the house. The van was parked until three-nineteen Tuesday morning when it reversed down the driveway. Then it swung right and slowly drove out of the camera range. The neighbor was emailing the video file. Jared was anxious to view it at the police station, on a bigger screen. Linda and I climbed off the hood as he headed around to the driver's door.

"See ya later," I said.

"What do you mean?"

I shrugged. "As in, we're going home. More than likely, we'll see you later."

"Don't you want to see the video?"

"You're going to let us tag along?"

Jared slid his sunglasses down his nose and looked over the frames at us. "We wouldn't have learned about this crime yet, or the one yesterday, if it wasn't for the two of you. With your help, we may be able to catch these guys soon and recover the goods. So get in the damn car. You can go with me to the station or I'll give you a ride home. Your choice."

Linda giggled and grabbed the handle for the front door. "Shotgun. Can I play with the siren on the way?"

"You're as bad as my kids," he muttered, climbing behind the wheel.

***

We went into a conference room at the station. On a big wall mounted screen, Jared pulled up the video from his email. Together we watched it several times at regular speed. Then we did it slowly, advancing the frames one at a time to get as much detail as we could. The lighting wasn't great. There was no natural light and no streetlights nearby. If there was supposed to be a light bulb above the license plate, it had been loosened or removed. We were about to view it again when Jared got a call. He didn't say much.

"We're checking to see if there are any merchants on

the main roads who have exterior security cameras. Unless the guy drove past one of those or a bank with an ATM camera, we may be out of luck."

Linda glanced at me. The initial excitement of discovery and being part of the investigation had worn off. It was already six o'clock. Jake was cooking dinner and expected us within half an hour. I picked up on her vibe.

"We should take off. Something tells me you're going to be at this a while," I said. "Can you give drive us home?"

Jared flashed a quick grin. "Arrangements have been made."

"What arrangements?" Linda asked.

The door to the conference room opened. Randy entered, beaming his crooked grin. "Your limousine awaits."

I leaned over and kissed Jared on the cheek. "Go get 'em, Columbo."

"Damn straight. Thanks again for your help. I've got patrol units checking rental homes on both sides of town. If we're lucky, we won't find any other crime scenes."

***

Jake insisted Randy stay for dinner. He had enough food for six people. There were grilled tuna steaks, potato wedges and a salad teeming with fresh produce. He'd even picked up a lemon meringue pie from a bakery near the farmer's market. We sat around the hexagonal picnic table, enjoying a leisurely meal. I thought Randy might be uncomfortable but he and Jake quickly hit it off. Logan entertained by fetching beers from the washtub. We filled in the guys on the day's discovery. Jake slowly shook his head.

"Sorry state of affairs. Kids breaking into people's houses like that. This isn't the big city. We don't get much crime. Ain't been a murder up here in forever."

"If it is kids, there's got to be someone else behind it. Somebody with more of a criminal background," I said.

"What makes you think so?" Randy asked.

"The artwork, for one. The fact that these guys are taking their time. Kids would break in, grab the booze and run. And they wouldn't be so thorough. From what Jared said, they haven't found any real fingerprints either. The prints they are able to get will likely belong to the homeowners."

Randy shrugged. "Kids watch a lot of television. They probably saw it on a detective show and have enough sense to wear gloves."

"I noticed that none of the homes have burglar alarms," Linda said. "Would kids know which houses to avoid?"

Jake had been quietly listening to the discussion. He finished his beer, smothered a belch and fired the empty can in the general direction of a recycling bin. It bounced off the side of the house, hit the rim and dropped in. As if on cue, Logan bounced up and trotted over to the washtub for a fresh one. He stood beside Jake with his tail waving like a pennant in the lake breeze. The dog dropped the can in the old man's outstretched hand and claimed his reward.

"Dog's smarter than most of the kids in this area. If there wasn't somebody behind them, they would have been caught robbing the first house."

"I think he's got a point," Randy said.

"Jared's got his work cut out for him," I said.

Linda wanted to spend some time with Logan. With a little persuasion, she dragged Jake along. He was reluctant to move, until she reminded him of the two divorcees he'd been dancing with last night. I offered to clean up after dinner. Randy pitched in. Working together, we had the leftovers put away and most of the dishes done quickly. I washed. He dried. The last plate was in my hands, deep in the sink filled with warm, soapy water. Randy's arms went around my waist and drew me close in a vertical spooning position.

"Ever done it in the kitchen," he whispered in my ear.

"Not this one. Don't get any ideas."

He was nuzzling my neck now. "Too late."

"They'll be back soon."

"How soon?"

Laughing, I pushed him away and flicked soap bubbles at him. "Forget it."

"Can't blame a guy for trying." He playfully snapped the towel at my ass. It was just damp enough to sting.

"Despite your efforts, my mind is still on the home invasions. There has got to be something we're missing."

Randy shrugged. "I'm not a cop or an investigative reporter. Nothing about this makes much sense."

I handed him the last dish and drained the sink. Through the window I could see Linda and Jake headed back. Randy gently set the plate in the cupboard and handed me the towel. "Think I'd better head out. Got a couple of things I need to do tonight."

Somehow we were standing together, arms around each other's waist. "Thanks for the ride home."

"Thank Jake for the dinner." He leaned in and kissed me, soft and gentle. "Can I see you tomorrow night?"

"What did you have in mind?"

He hesitated, looking up at the ceiling. "I don't know. But we can make it memorable."

"Dinner?"

"Sure." We started kissing again. Only when I heard Logan bark outside did I push Randy away. Letting him go had become more difficult.

"I'll meet you at the boat." My voice was a little shaky.

"Six-thirty. And Jamie…"

"Yeah?"

"Bring your jammies."

With a nod, he went out the door. I stayed by the sink, waiting for my heartbeat to return to a normal rhythm. Through the screen, I heard Randy say goodnight to the others. This whole vacation was filled with unexpected turns. First, the robberies, then the romance. Or was it the other way around? It all seemed so odd. Maybe Linda was right. I was overdue for attention from a nice guy. She must have caught my vibe, because Linda walked into the kitchen and grabbed a bottle of wine from the refrigerator.

"You look like you're off in fantasyland."

"More like wonderland."

She poured two generous servings in plastic cups. "As in you're wondering how this is all going to play out?"

I nodded. "It's a fling. Nothing more. We both know it. There's no chance I'm moving from Motown to pursue this."

"So enjoy it. Don't overthink it. You've caught the eye of a handsome man who wants to spend time with you. Isn't that good enough?"

"You're right." I took one of the cups and we went outside to relax with Jake. But in the back of my mind, I kept wondering if it was too good to be true.

CHAPTER SIX

Friday morning, we headed to the beach early. We had anticipated a larger crowd, with many of the weekend people arriving before dinner. After some sun, we splashed in the lake. The water was already getting busy and it wasn't even noon. There was plenty of noise to distract us. Speedboats cruised parallel to the shore. Sailboats headed out of the marina. Surfers using kites were zooming about, turning tricks with the waves and wind. There was a buzzing noise that would rise and fade, but I didn't give it much thought.

We sprawled on our backs. Even through the towel, I felt the warmth of the sand. Linda was talking about the book she'd been reading when she started laughing.

"I think we have a secret admirer."

I looked around the beach but didn't see anyone paying attention to us. Linda brushed her fingers across my forearm and pointed directly above. About thirty feet overhead was a drone. Four little propellers spun about, holding it steady. There was a camera attached to the undercarriage. Linda pressed her lips together and blew a kiss. The little craft shifted, then moved along the beach.

"An electronic peeping Tom. I wonder how long that's

been following us."

A little jolt of electricity went through me. "What the hell."

She propped up on an elbow and looked at me. "It's probably just some kid screwing around. You weren't flashing your boobs at him were you?"

"I don't care. When did you notice it?"

"Jamie, they've been around all week. That was the closest one's been. But they fly all over the place. I've seen them in town, at the marina, and even at the concert the other night. What's the big deal?"

I pointed at the drone. "Can we follow it? I really want to talk to the guy behind the controls."

"The peeping Tom thing was a joke."

I already moved down the sand. She scrambled off the towels and fell into step beside me. "Jamie, you do realize chasing the drone won't necessarily lead us to its owner."

Linda made sense, but I was reluctant to listen. I watched as the machine went another few yards down the shore and circled back toward us. It hovered, still about thirty feet above the ground. I extended both arms and waved it toward me with my hands. It moved closer.

"What's going on?"

"I've got an idea." Dropping to the sand, I began smoothing it out. "Help me."

Linda shrugged. Then she knelt beside me and mimicked my efforts. When there was a large square I used my forefinger and wrote a message in foot high letters. The drone was lower now. I got to my feet and pulled Linda up beside me. We watched the craft shift, moving closer. It was less than twenty feet now. It circled the area. The camera was right above us. Then it dropped down a few feet and went back up. Twice. I waved and it took off. Linda stared as I wiped out the message with my feet.

"Did you just make a date with a drone?"

"Yep. Now move your cute little ass. We don't want to keep him waiting."

"Jamie, this guy could be four feet tall and six hundred pounds. What are you thinking?"

"I'm thinking this gives us a lead. And that ice cream on a hot summer day sounds good."

Captain Nemo's restaurant was right on Phoenix Street by the entrance to the marina. It's a small diner, with burgers and fries and a large variety of ice cream. Neither one of us were big on ice cream, but it was the first spot that came to mind.

We were in front of the store, sitting on a bench. It was packed inside. There was no guarantee the drone operator would show up. But if there was a chance we could get answers to some questions, I was willing to wait. Linda people watched, mumbling a commentary, starting with a hefty old guy wearing shorts and a Hawaiian shirt.

"Not this one, he looks incapable of operating anything beyond a bottle opener."

"Be nice," I whispered.

"You dragged me away from the beach. I don't have to be nice."

"He's not the type to play with a drone."

"They have a type?"

I shrugged. "Just a guess. I'm thinking nerdy guys, more interested in computers and science than anything else. Except maybe looking at girls. Not talking to them or touching them, just looking at them."

"You're terrible."

That earned her another shrug. We watched people parade by. There were a lot of families on the sidewalks, along with plenty of couples of all ages. Whoever was behind the controls knew what we looked like. Linda started to fidget. This wasn't exactly a stakeout. But my curiosity wouldn't leave it alone. I'd wait another ten minutes before giving up.

That's when two teenage kids arrived. They were young, thirteen or fourteen years old. Gangly, with arms and legs that seemed to go on forever. Both were in shorts and tank tops. The strawberry-blonde wore a ponytail. The brunette had on a worn Tigers baseball cap. And they were girls.

Linda looked them over and faced me. "You were saying?"

"Shut up." I stuck out a hand. "I'm Jamie. This is Linda. We just want to talk to you about the drone."

"Morgan," said the strawberry-blonde as she shook my hand. "This is Kelly. We were just experimenting with it. My dad would kill me if he found out we've been using it."

"We're not going to tell anybody. I just want to know how it works."

Linda picked up on the anxiety. Teaching in high school helped her recognize and deal with teenage angst. "Kelly and I will get in line for the ice cream. That will give you two time to talk about …drones."

Once they moved away, Morgan settled onto the bench. She explained her father and older brother liked to fly it along the beach. They would practice maneuvers, get video of the various boats and people and even some great sunsets. The camera could be linked to a cell phone or a computer, which made it easy to watch from a distance. She and Kelly were best friends. They were in the local STEM program. As such, they were curious about technology. Morgan admitted that while her dad and brother liked to 'mess around' with the drone, she and Kelly were better at operating it. They were only supposed to use it with a parent's supervision.

"But we're bored. There are a bunch of drones flying around anyway. Nobody is going to tell ours apart from the others. We just wanted to fly it out this morning. We didn't mean to bother you."

An obvious question jumped to mind. "Do you fly it just along the beach?"

"Mostly. We take off from my backyard. It's a couple of blocks up from the lake. So we get high enough to avoid the power lines and trees, then it's a clear shot to the water. We use my laptop, since the screen is bigger." Morgan became more animated, describing the technology and her abilities at the controls.

I learned more in the fifteen minutes from Morgan than I ever thought I'd learn about drones. She taught me about how the drone operated, how far it could fly and obstacles they had to be aware of before Linda and Kelly returned. Each carried a waffle cone packed with ice cream. Linda handed over the Mackinac Island fudge to Morgan.

"You didn't bring me one?" I asked with a sly smile.

"You're welcome to go stand in line. But ice cream is no substitute for lunch. And it's your turn to buy. Did you get what you needed?"

"Almost." I turned to Morgan. "Can we get a quick demonstration?"

She and Kelly exchanged a glance. Kelly was working her way through a scoop of moose tracks. "Sure. We can show you the beach and the shoreline."

"That's good, but I have something else in mind."

Linda wasn't quite ready to move on. "When you were flying over the beach this morning, why did you hover above us?"

Kelly glanced down. Her cheeks flushed in embarrassment. "I was teasing her."

"About what? Us?"

"No, it was more about us."

My confusion was evident. "What do you mean?"

Kelly wiggled a couple of fingers at Linda and I, then swung her hand around and pointed and herself and Morgan. "I told her if we were lucky, we'd end up looking like you two. You know, one redhead, one brunette. Rocking the bikinis and owning the beach."

Linda released a bawdy laugh. "That is the sweetest thing I've heard in a long time. Have you two been friends long?"

"Practically all our lives. Since second grade."

She slipped an arm over Kelly's shoulders. "First grade for us. I'll bet Morgan is the troublemaker. Very inquisitive. Always wants to push it, right up to the edge of when you might get caught."

"How did you know?"

Linda winked. "Redheads. C'mon, let's go see this drone. Then Jamie's buying lunch for you guys, too."

"All right!"

***

After the demonstration and lunch, we headed back to the beach. Our favorite spot was no longer available, so we moved away from the growing crowd. Linda sprawled face down and I covered her bronzed skin with the sunscreen. I sat cross-legged. From my bag I dug out a small notebook and a pencil.

"Seriously?" she mumbled.

"Just a couple of things to plot out. It's coming together now."

"Or unraveling. Don't you need your rest before your big date tonight?"

Randy. This morning's discovery had pushed him out of my mind temporarily. But I was close to putting all the pieces together. I could hand it over to Jared and let him wrap it up. If he believed me. I didn't know who, but mostly knew how. That was the foundation for any good story. From there, it was a matter of filling in the gaps. Frustrated, I tossed the book aside and stretched out beside her.

"Morgan and Kelly were kind of cute," I said.

"Like looking in a mirror fifteen years ago."

"Please. You were never gangly. You had those curves when you were ten years old."

She gave me a warm smile. "I was eleven. And you've probably had that inquisitive nature and stubborn streak since the day you were born."

"You'll have to ask Vera for confirmation on that."

"So where is your globetrotting mother this week?"

I shrugged. "Not sure. It was either the Hamptons, Montreal or Boston. She had several offers from friends to visit their *rustic* summer homes."

"She doesn't know what she's missing."

My mother traveled through high society like a butterfly on a summer's breeze. We connect with occasional phone calls and emails. It's not the typical relationship, but we're accustomed to it. The last time I saw her was last year on Labor Day.

Linda and I relaxed in the sun. If this wasn't paradise, it was pretty damn close. Best friends sharing a vacation, with warm sand, gentle breezes, ample sunshine and great food. Mix in some friendly people. Add a little romance. Damn near perfect. Conversation faded. We dozed. There were times when it seemed Linda and I could communicate without words through a comfortable silence. At length, we walked down for a quick swim.

"So are you going to share your theory with Jared?" Linda's curls were dotted with water. The sunlight made them sparkle.

"Yeah, but he may not want to hear it."

Playfully she smacked my shoulder. "He's not a caveman. The guy has been receptive to your meddling so far."

"Sure. I'll give him a call."

Back on the towels, she pulled her phone from the bag. Before I could change my mind, Linda handed it over. Jared was on the other end. He listened without interruption as I laid it out. When I was done, he gave me specific instructions and disconnected. Linda watched me closely.

"He wants to meet us. Fifteen minutes at the park where the concert was."

She smiled sweetly. "Is he bringing lover-boy with him?"

"Shut up."

Laughing, we packed up our gear and left the beach.

***

Randy was with him. He started to reach for me but a look from Jared stopped him. Sheepishly, he shrugged.

"He bumped into me as I was leaving the office. My mistake was telling him who I was meeting." Jared gave his head a slow shake. "He followed me out to the car, like a puppy chasing after a new toy."

"That's sounds like an appropriate analogy," Linda said.

"I'm a new toy?"

"Hush," Linda replied, "let's hear what Jared has in mind."

For a few weeks now, the police department had been getting complaints of drones flying through different neighborhoods. The patrol units had been alerted, but unless they happened upon someone operating the controls, there wasn't much they could do. We were standing around a picnic table under the gazebo. Randy drifted over and bumped my hip with his. Maybe he was a puppy.

"Do you know the areas where the drones were spotted?" I asked.

Jared considered it, then pulled out his phone and called the dispatcher. While waiting for the details, he sent Randy back to the car to get the map. He spread it open on the table while Jared finished the conversation.

"You're on to something again, Jamie. Each of the homes broken into was in an area where we got complaints. A couple claimed a drone came through several times and flew lower around some of the houses. Before we were able to get there, the drone was gone. So this is how they're doing recon." Jared took a red pen and circled the different neighborhoods on the map.

Linda leaned over the table. "Are there any complaints

outside these areas?"

"Two," Jared said. He noted those on the map as well. "Opposite ends of the territory."

"So those are targets," I said.

"Makes sense. I need to go talk with the residents who called in. See if they can pinpoint which houses the drones were focused on." Jared tapped his forefinger on the map as he considered something. The rest of us waited. At length, he gave his head a shake and looked away. "I must be out of my mind."

"Ask us," Linda said.

"Ask us what?" Randy said.

"Ask us to help," Linda said. "We're already neck deep in this. What are you thinking?"

Jared cleared his throat. "We've got a small police force and a handful of reserves. Friday nights and weekends during the summer require us to put damn near every able body out on the streets. Keeping the tourists safe is a priority."

"You're thinking of a stakeout?" I offered.

"Yeah. Two neighborhoods. We have a general idea what the van looks like. If I can narrow it down, we might get lucky. Catch the van and the thieves in the act."

"We're not cops," Randy said, choosing his words carefully. "We're not trained for this kind of thing."

"So you sit in a car and watch. If you see the van, you call me. I'll scramble the others. We know from the video these guys take their time."

"And they don't go in until well after dark," I pointed out.

Linda and I exchanged a glance. "We're in."

"I'm going to check those neighborhoods. We should be in position by 9:30." Jared folded the map and tucked it in his back pocket. His glanced flicked to Randy. "Are you in or out? I need to know. Right now."

Jared was an intimidating guy. Randy met his gaze and didn't waver. "I'm in."

"Let's go. We've got work to do."

We watched the two guys drive away. Linda gave me a coy smile.

"What?"

"Looks like your pajama party just got cancelled."

I huffed out a breath in frustration. "Aw, what the hell."

CHAPTER SEVEN

The guys arrived at Jake's shortly after 9:00. Once the sun was gone, it got chilly off the lake. Both neighborhoods were not far from the water, however I didn't know what the appropriate fashions were for a stake out. We opted for comfort. Linda and I had changed into jeans, sneakers and T-shirts. Jake acknowledged the two men with a nod. Jared grinned, then reached down and scrubbed Logan between the ears.

"Ready to roll?" he asked.

"Yes indeed," Linda said. "What's your plan?"

His eyes flicked to Jake. "You think those two can be trusted to pay attention?"

"I can't vouch for Blondie, but Strawberry Shortcake there ain't gonna be distracted. She's stubborn. These break-ins are pissing her off. Lousy people stealing haven."

"Strawberry shortcake?" I asked.

Jake grinned and raised his shoulders to his ears. "First thing that came to mind. You are kinda sweet, too."

I didn't know whether to pissed or pleased. The fact that Linda was laughing loudly didn't help matters any. Jared was beside her, doing his best to hold back a grin. He looked down at the dog for a moment. "How about you and me in my car. Bring the pup. We'll take the northern site."

"You're gonna trust me with Strawberry Shortcake?" Randy asked.

"Something tells me she'll keep you in line. Keep your phones handy. Let's roll."

As we walked to the car, Randy slid an arm around my waist. I glanced at him in the fading light. He was biting his lip, no doubt to hold back a laugh or a comment. Time to nip this in the bud.

"Call me Strawberry Shortcake one more time, and you can forget about sex or ever seeing me naked again."

His hand dipped down and squeezed my ass. "Yes, ma'am. But you are kinda sweet."

"Shut up."

We were quiet on the drive over. My nerves were dancing with anticipation. There was a good chance we might catch the bad guys. He backed into the driveway of a nearby house and killed the lights. We were set far enough back from the road that we were invisible to passing cars. On the back seat was a cooler with some water bottles, cookies and energy bars. We cracked the windows to let some air in.

"Wanna neck?" Randy asked as his right hand slid up my leg.

"Maybe later."

"We could fool around." His hand crept higher.

"Apparently I've unleashed a hormonal monster. Behave. Stay focused on the house. If we're lucky, you might get lucky."

He didn't move his hand any higher, but he didn't pull it away either. "Something to hope for. Jared said if they don't strike by two in the morning, we'll hang it up."

We reclined the seats a bit. Conversation drifted to stories about our childhoods and families. An hour passed by quickly. Then second one dragged. I was too keyed up to doze. Randy yawned. We split a pack of Oreos. My phone buzzed. Linda, checking in.

"Quiet over here. We're going for a walk," she said.

"Good idea. We'll do the same."

"Keep your phone on. And stay out of the bushes."

"No promises."

Randy had switched off the dome lights earlier. Now we eased from the truck and made our way down the street. With arms around each other, we looked like any other couple, out for a late evening stroll. I wondered if Linda was copying my position with Jared. Walking the dog would be great cover. No one would suspect anything unusual there. We turned a corner and made our way around the block. The feel of Randy's hand on my waist and his arm around me had become quite natural. I tried not to think about what we might have been doing right then if we weren't on the stakeout.

Midnight came and went. I began to have some doubts when headlights appeared at the end of the block. Before they got passed the corner, they winked out.

"You see that?"

Randy nodded. We stayed low, watching the dark vehicle move closer. I held my breath as they pulled into the driveway of the target house. It was a dark van, just like the one we'd seen on the video. There was no brake or taillights showing. The bulb above the license plate didn't work either. Randy called Jared.

"Do *not* approach them. We'll be there in two minutes."

"We're not going anywhere," Randy said.

Two minutes felt like twenty. Then we watched Jared's big sedan roll into place across the bottom of the driveway. He slid from behind the wheel. Out of the shadows two uniformed officers appeared. We'd learn later that they had already blocked the street at both ends with patrol cars. Other officers were waiting there. Jared and the other cops approached the house slowly. To my amazement, Linda slipped out of the car. Logan followed and sat beside her.

"Let's go." I popped the door and started moving. Randy was right with me. Just as we got across the street, all hell broke loose. Lights blazed in the house. Flashlight beams danced around. A door slammed and we heard someone running. Jared must have found a switch inside, because suddenly spotlights came on, filling the yard with light. One police officer was chasing a guy. The guy spun around and whipped something in the general direction of the cop. He staggered and went to his knees. The guy turned away.

Linda had been kneeling beside Logan, her right hand gripping his collar. She extended her left arm up the driveway. "Capture!" The dog bolted.

"Wait here!" Randy shouted, chasing after the dog.

"Fuck that!" I glanced at Linda but she was already moving up the driveway, heading toward the fallen officer. I raced after Randy.

Up ahead I heard someone scream. Lights came on in other yards. There was a lot of noise and confusion. But beneath it all, I heard a familiar guttural growl. Rounding the corner of a house, I saw Logan. He stood over a guy who was flat on his back, trying to squirm away from the dog. Logan's jaws were clamped around an arm. It didn't look like he was ever letting go.

"Get him off me!"

Randy hesitated. Logan held his ground. Shadows danced through the yard lights. Jared appeared beside me. "Damn, I love that dog. How do you make him stop?"

We moved up beside the guy's head. In the light, I could see that Logan hadn't broken the skin, but his vice-like grip was keeping the guy in place. "Release!" The dog's jaws moved as if he was yawning and he stepped back.

The guy tried to scramble backward on his butt.

Jared loomed above him. "Going somewhere?"

CHAPTER EIGHT

Sunset over Lake Michigan was breathtaking. I was behind the wheel, heading back toward the marina. Linda and Jake were on the rear bench. Logan was sprawled before them. Randy sat in the passenger seat, a beer can dangling from his fingers. The day had been busy but the evening was relaxing. After an early dinner at Jake's, we'd gone for a long cruise along the lake. Randy was comfortable with me at the helm. But I'd let him bring it back to the dock.

As we tied up, I noticed four people walking toward the pier. Stepping from the shadows were Jared and Sara with two young girls. Logan scrambled out of the boat and went to greet them. We followed.

"Thought you'd all want the update. I had to bribe the girls with ice cream," Jared said.

Sara linked an arm through his. "It didn't take much convincing."

Jared gave us the details. It was a three-man crew doing the break-ins. Using the drone, they scouted areas, avoiding homes of permanent residents. With the camera, they'd look through windows, finding likely targets. Two of the men were young, early twenties, without permanent jobs. The third guy had a criminal record for robbery and possession of stolen goods. He had been renting a house outside of town. A search of the house and shed led to the recovery of many of the stolen items. Jared would receive a commendation for busting the gang. There was a small chance we would have to come back and testify if there was a trial. Jared felt the crew would take a plea deal.

"How's the other officer?" Linda asked.

"Slight concussion. The guy threw a crowbar at him. He deflected most of it with his arm, but still got quite a knot in his forehead. He's getting a lot of sympathy from his girlfriend."

Jared wrapped up everything. Then Sara and his daughters succeeded in dragging him back toward town. After an exchange of goodnight hugs and kisses, Linda, Jake and Logan followed. At long last, Randy and I were alone. His arms drew me close.

"When do you leave?"

"We need to be on the road by noon. Gotta go back to work on Monday."

"Did you bring your jammies?"

"Knew I forgot something!"

"Guess you'll just have to sleep naked." He leaned in. A long, slow kiss followed.

Randy guided me down below. We both knew tonight would be our last. So much had transpired during the week. There was no chance of anything happening beyond that. But there was tonight. The gentle breeze from the lake, the rocking of the boat in its dock and two people wrapped up together, even if was only for a few hours. It didn't get much better than that.

Paradise.

The End

ACKNOWLEDGEMENTS

Special thanks to Melissa Keir for her amazing editing skills and never-ending support. And to Annette, Bill, Jerry, Peg and all the rest of the Stormy Night Writer's Group for all of their encouragement. You guys rock!

CHECK OUT THE REST OF THE JAMIE RICHMOND SERIES…

Grab hold of your seat as amateur sleuth, Jamie Richmond sets out to find the shooter of a local police trooper. She puts her life and heart on the line...Devious is the first in a gripping mystery series by local Michigan author.

~~~

Jamie Richmond, reporter turned author, is doing research for her next book. Attempting to capture the realism of a police officer's duties while on patrol, she manages to tag along for a shift with a state trooper. A few traffic stops and a high speed chase later, Jamie's ride takes an unexpected turn when she witnesses the trooper being shot.

Although it is not a fatal injury, Jamie becomes obsessed with unraveling the facts behind this violent act. While she is trying to sort out this puzzle, she becomes romantically involved with Malone, another trooper with a few mysteries of his own. Now Jamie's attention is divided between a blooming romance and solving the crime which
~~~

is haunting her.

Jamie begins to question the events that took place and exactly who could be behind the shooting. It was a devious mind. But who?

~~~

When Jamie's best friend vanishes, she'll do anything to find her and bring her home.

A new year marks new beginnings for Jamie Richmond. Not only has she moved into a cozy new house, but she's brought Malone along with her to fan the flames of their growing romance. When Jamie's best friend, Linda Davis, enters the picture, she thinks everything is right with the world.

Linda begins a May-September romance with Vincent Schulte, Jamie's doctor and good friend. But while Vince is sweeping Linda off her feet, she unknowingly has captured the attention of a stalker. The idyllic life suddenly takes a very bad turn when Linda disappears without a trace on a cold and snowy day. The police are scrambling to find a clue that will lead them to Linda.

Malone does his best to comfort Jamie and encourages her to let the professionals do their job. But if there's one thing he's learned in their time together, it's
~~~

that nothing will stop this stubborn redhead from solving t mystery.

Jamie turns all of her attention on figuring out who took Linda and where she might be, regardless of the dangers she may face. Her efforts once again put her in harm's way. But will she find her best friend?

~~~

A discovery of priceless artwork leads Jamie on a collision course with danger.

Jamie Richmond used to live a nice, quiet life. But last fall she witnessed the shooting of a police officer and figured out who did it. Then this winter saw her best friend targeted by a stalker and kidnapped. Yep, Jamie solved that one and came to the rescue. Now it's summertime and the living is supposed to be easy. All she wants to do is write her novels and spend free time with Malone, the guy who has been by her side since all this craziness began. But that's not likely to happen.

Jamie's father was a very successful sculptor who tragically died more than twenty years ago when she was just a child. What she remembers about him is little more than bits and pieces. A storeroom filled with crates of his work is discovered in an old converted factory. This
~~~

potential fortune in artwork has been waiting all these years.

Jamie recruits Malone and a few close friends to help her unpack the crates and bring her father's gifts out to the light of day. News of this discovery leads to a robbery. Now Jamie is determined to figure out who is behind the crime.

ABOUT THE AUTHOR

Mark Love (yes, that's really his name) lived for many years in the metropolitan Detroit area, where crime and corruption are always prevalent. A former freelance reporter, Love is drawn to mysteries and the twists and turns that mirror real life. He is the author of three books in the Jamie Richmond Series "Devious" "Vanishing Act" and "Fleeing Beauty" and The Jefferson Chene Series "WHY 319?", "Your Turn to Die", and soon to be released "The Wayward Path" and several short stories.

Love resides in west Michigan with his wife, Kim. He enjoys a wide variety of music, reading and writing fiction, cooking, travel, most sports and the great outdoors. You can find his blog at the link below and on Goodreads, Facebook, and Amazon.

http://www.amazon.com/-/e/B009P7HVZQ

http:// motownmysteries.blogspot.com/

https://www.facebook.com/MarkLoveAuthor

https://twitter.com/motownmysteries

https://www.instagram.com/motownmysteries/

www.ingramcontent.com/pod-product-compliance
Ingram Content Group UK Ltd.
Pitfield, Milton Keynes, MK11 3LW, UK
UKHW041844200726
13854UKWH00005BA/2063

9 781953 335708